For Toby – JW
For Luke – GP

Crabtree Publishing Company
www.crabtreebooks.com

PMB 16A, 350 Fifth Avenue,
Suite 3308,
New York, NY
10118

612 Welland Avenue,
St. Catharines,
Ontario, Canada
L2M 5V6

Published by Crabtree Publishing Company in 2004
Published in 2001 by Random House Children's Books and Red Fox

Cataloging-in-Publication data

Waite, Judy.
  Digging for Dinosaurs / written by judy Waite ; illustrated by
Garry Parsons.
      p. cm. – (Flying foxes)
  Summary: Dan learns about dinosaurs and the true value of
museums in helping people learn about the past
  ISBN 0-7787-1483-7 (RLB) – ISBN 0-7787-1529-9 (PB)
  [1. Natural History–Fiction. 2. Family–Fiction.] I. Parsons, Gary
ill. II. Title. III. Series.

2003022714
LC

Text copyright © Judy Waite 2001
Illustrations copyright © Garry Parsons 2001

Set in Cheltenham Book Infant

1 2 3 4 5 6 7 8 9 0 Printed and bound in Malaysia by Tien Wah Press 0 9 8 7 6 5 4 3

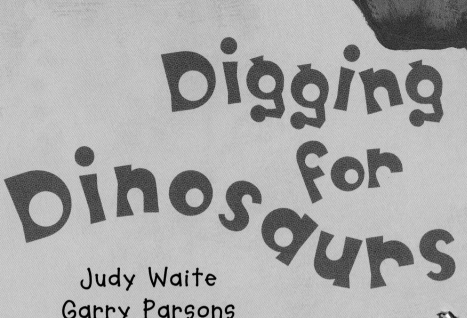

Digging for Dinosaurs

Judy Waite

Garry Parsons

Dan was reading his favorite book.
"I want to dig for dinosaurs,"
he said suddenly.

Dan's dog, Bouncer, bounced over to him.
Dan ruffled Bouncer's ears.

"Let's start in the backyard," he said.

"Don't get muddy," warned Dan's mom. "I've planned a trip to the museum."

Dan didn't answer. He knew he'd hate the museum. Museums were musty, smelly, and dusty.

Soon Dan was digging a deep, dark hole.
"I'm going two hundred and twenty-five
million years deep," he told Bouncer.

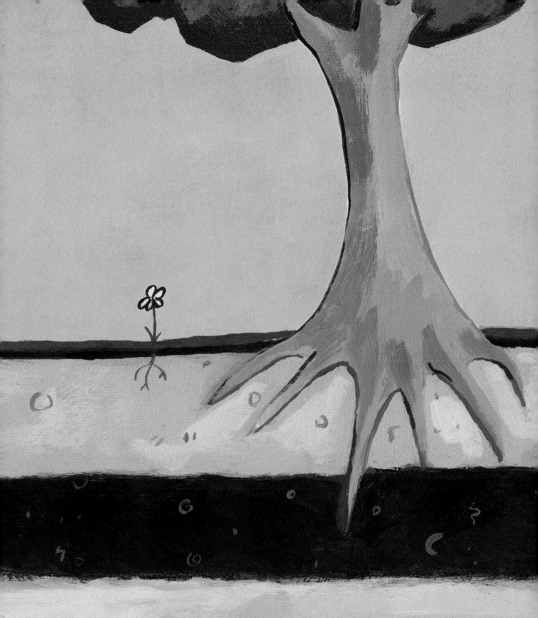

He felt a bubble of excitement. Wouldn't
it be great to really find a dinosaur?
He wondered if he'd recognize it if he did.

Bouncer scratched
at the edge of the
hole. A sprinkle of
mud slid back into it.

"Don't do that," groaned Dan. "I've just dug down to the Cretaceous period. I might be about to find the remains of a terrible Tyrannosaurus rex that could swallow a boy in just two bites."

The hole grew
deeper and darker.

Dan found a
stone – like an
odd sort of bone.

But he didn't find the remains of a terrible
Tyrannosaurus rex that could swallow a
boy in just two bites.

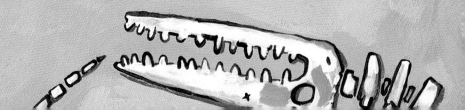

Dan's mom called to him, "We're going in ten minutes!"

We're going in ten minutes!

Dan growled
his grumpiest
Tyrannosaurus growl.

He threw the odd
looking stone for
Bouncer to chase.
Museums were
boring. Like old
people snoring.

15

Bouncer came bouncing
back. He dropped the
stone into the hole.
A slither of mud
trickled down
on top of it.

"Don't do that," groaned Dan. "I've just dug down to the Jurassic period. I might be about to find the remains of a gigantic Brachiosaurus that was taller than the tallest trees."

Dan kept on
digging. The hole
grew deeper
and darker.

Dan found
a peg, and
a pin,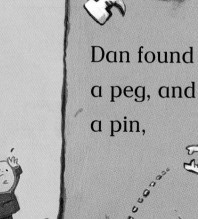

and a
scrunched-up old tin.

But he didn't find the remains of a gigantic Brachiosaurus that was taller than the tallest trees.

"I hope you're not getting too mucky," called his mom. "We're going in five minutes."

Dan stamped his foot like a bad-tempered Brachiosaurus. He threw the odd looking stone for Bouncer to chase.

Museums were sleepy, crummy, and creepy.

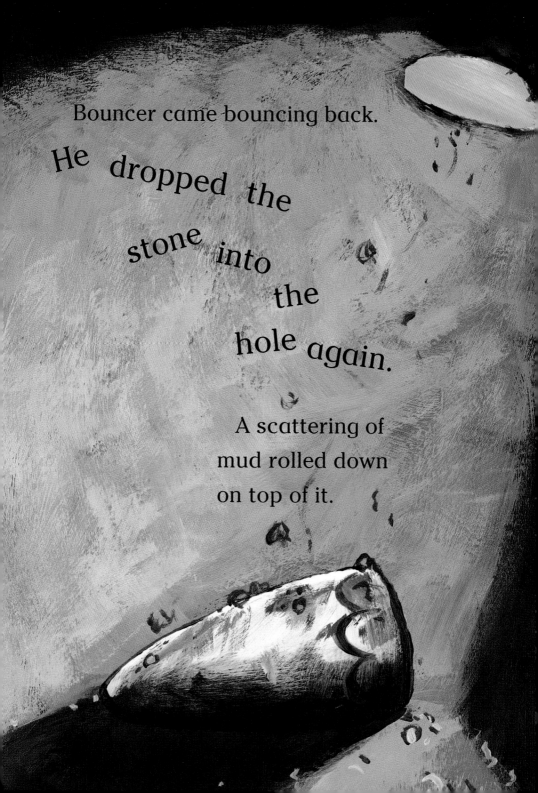

Bouncer came bouncing back.

He dropped the
stone into
the
hole again.

A scattering of
mud rolled down
on top of it.

"Don't do that," groaned Dan. "I've just dug all the way down to the Triassic period. I might be about to find the remains of the crazy Coelophysis that had knife-sharp teeth and sometimes ate its own young."

Dan kept on digging. The hole grew deeper and darker.

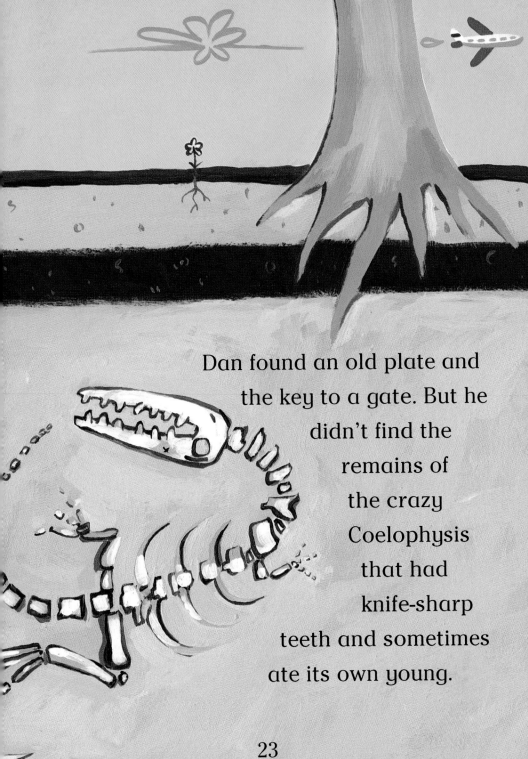

Dan found an old plate and the key to a gate. But he didn't find the remains of the crazy Coelophysis that had knife-sharp teeth and sometimes ate its own young.

Dan's mom appeared suddenly. "You're covered in mud," she said angrily. "Go inside and get cleaned up. It's time to go."

Dan made his craziest Coelophysis face.
He threw the odd looking stone
for Bouncer to chase.
Museums were old,
crusty, and cold.

Bouncer came bouncing back. He dropped the stone into the hole again. A shower of mud pattered down on top of it.

"Come on, Dan," said his mom. Dan growled and stamped and gnashed his dinosaur teeth.

Then he turned to Bouncer,
"Go on, bury your bone
in my hole. Digging for
dinosaurs was a stupid
idea anyway."

He stomped away into the house.

In the bathroom, Dan stared into the mirror. He had a front tooth missing, and he stuck his tongue through the gap.

He thought about how some dinosaurs grew new teeth when the old ones broke.

Then he practiced his angry dinosaur face in the mirror.

Dan's mom peered around the door, "Hurry up!" she grumbled.

Dan's mom drove to the museum. Dan
looked out of the back window
and imagined a world
full of dinosaurs.

He pictured them wandering wild
among vast mountains and plains.

He heard snorts. He heard roars.

He saw great
grabbing claws . . .

"We're here," said Dan's mom, pulling
into the museum parking lot.
Dan trailed behind his mom
into the museum.

And when he got inside – he was surprised.

No one was bored, nobody snored. No one was sleepy, nothing seemed creepy.

It wasn't cold, and it wasn't old.
It was all fresh and new,
with zillions to do.

It had fossils
and stones . . .

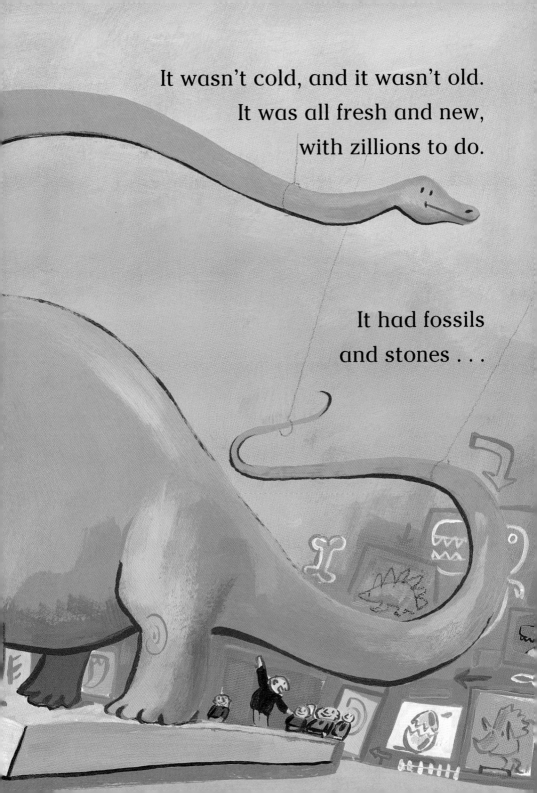

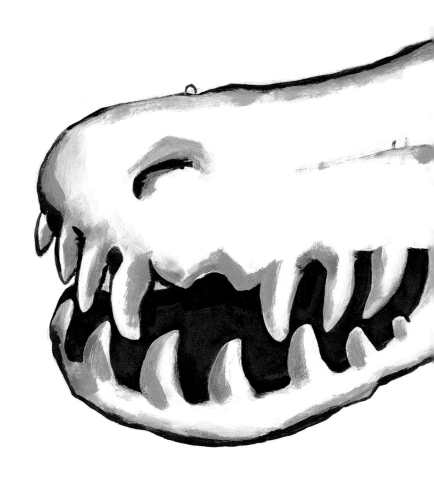

. . . and some very large bones.

Dan stared and stared
at the Tyrannosaurus rex.
Monster sized questions
rose up in his mind.

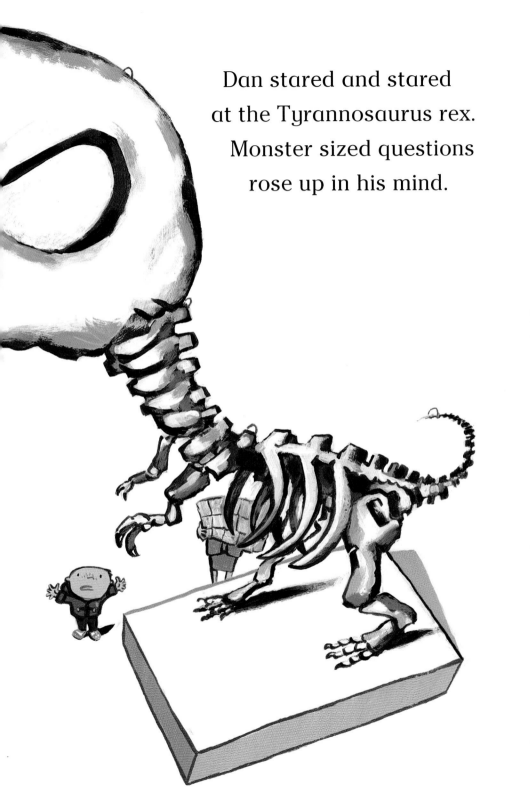

How fast could it run?

How loud did
it roar?

What would it be like to see those giant
jaws really begin to open . . .

"Just look at those fearsome fangs,"
said Dan's mom.

"There's one missing!" cried Dan.
"It's got a gap in its mouth –
just like me."

Dan could see the sort of shape the missing tooth would be. He could see the sort of size the missing tooth would be.

He gave his mom his most gigantic dinosaur smile, "I've had a great time, but we have to go home. I've got to dig up an odd looking stone . . ."

Can you help Dan make a T-rex skeleton like the one in the museum? What others can you make?

You will need: nine pipe cleaners

1. HEAD, BODY, AND TAIL: twist the ends of two pipe cleaners together and shape into a curve.

2. TOP OF HEAD: curve the end of the first pipe cleaner around. Shape into zigzag teeth.

3. LOWER JAW: zigzag the end of a pipe cleaner into teeth and loop it under. Twist the long end onto the body.

4. FRONT LEGS: fold a pipe cleaner in half and join its middle onto the body just below the head. Fold the ends in half again.

5. RIBS: twist three pipe cleaners into circles. Cross the ends over and twist them onto the body.

6. BACK LEGS: twist two pipe cleaners onto either side of the body. Shape the ends into flat feet with three toes so that your dinosaur stands up.

*Hint: make sure you wind the pipe cleaners tightly around each other!

Massive head with large jaws to crush prey

Tiny arms

Powerful legs

I eat plant-eating dinosaurs. Yum, yum!

T-rex Tooth
(As long as a grown-up's hand)

Pointed teeth with sharp edges like saws were good for eating meat. Dinosaur teeth grew back when they wore down.

Tyrannosaurus rex (tie-ranna-saw-rus rex) was one of the largest meat eaters. It was a carnosaur, or "flesh lizard." It was so heavy it couldn't run fast for very long. It waited for its prey and attacked quickly.

> Meet the author.

Judy Waite

How did you get the idea for this story? When my two daughters were young, they loved digging for treasure. They found all kinds of things – odd-shaped stones, buttons, tins . . . They would bring their treasure home and play 'museum.' We also had a dog called Clarrie, who loved chasing sticks and burying them. These memories gave me the idea for this story. Then I went to the library and found out all about dinosaurs.

Did you write when you were little? I have always loved writing. I grew up in a country called Singapore, and because it was so hot, we only had to go to school in the mornings. I think having all that time to play helped my imagination to grow, so I thought up a lot of stories.

Can I be a writer like you? Don't wait until your teacher asks for a story – write for your mom, your little brother, or even your goldfish. Make comics. Read a lot. Enter story writing competitions. The more you write, the better you will be.

Garry Parsons

How did you do the pictures in this book? The pictures are painted in acrylic paints, with some colored pencil scribbles. I painted all the pictures at the same time and they took four weeks non-stop to finish.

Did you know all about dinosaurs? Yes, I loved dinosaurs when I was young, especially Tyrannosaurus rex and Diplodocus. I liked comparing their sizes to buses and people and imagining them in the yard.

Have you ever seen a dinosaur skeleton? Yes, in the Natural History Museum in London, England. It's like the museum Dan visits and has a lot of dinosaurs you can see close-up.

What did you like to do when you were a child? I liked to imagine volcanoes erupting in the yard, and to make things from scraps of paper.

How can I be an illustrator like you? Take a notebook everywhere and draw. Imagine dinosaurs in your street – draw them!

Will you try and write or draw a story?

47

Let your ideas take flight with

Flying Foxes

Digging for Dinosaurs
by Judy Waite and Garry Parsons

Only Tadpoles Have Tails
by Jane Clarke and Jane Gray

The Magic Backpack
by Julia Jarman and Adriano Gon

Slow Magic
by Pippa Goodhart and John Kelly

Sherman Swaps Shells
by Jane Clarke and Ant Parker

That's Not Right!
by Alan Durant and Katharine McEwen